# ABC LONDON

James Dunn
Illustrated by Kate Slater

F
FRANCES LINCOLN
CHILDREN'S BOOKS

A is for
Art

For Hector and Aurora with love and thanks to Phoebe — J.D.
For Ronley, with love — K.S.

**ABC London** copyright © Frances Lincoln Limited 2012
Text copyright © James Dunn 2012
Illustrations copyright © Kate Slater 2012
The right of Kate Slater to be identified as the illustrator of this work has been asserted by her
in accordance with the Copyright, Designs and Patents Act, 1988 (United Kingdom).

First published in Great Britain in 2012 by
Frances Lincoln Children's Books, 4 Torriano Mews,
Torriano Avenue, London NW5 2RZ
www.franceslincoln.com

A catalogue record for this book is available from the British Library.

ISBN 978-1-84780-297-2

Illustrated with paper collage

Printed in Printed in Dongguan, Guangdong, China by Toppan Leefung in February 2012

1 3 5 7 9 8 6 4 2

C is for
Changing the Guard

**D** is for
Dick
Whittington

**E**is for Elephant and Castle

F is for Fashion

# G is for Gherkin

# H

is for

## HAMPSTEAD HEATH

I IS FOR ISLE OF DOGS

**J**

**is for**

**Jewels**

# K is for King's Cross

King's Cross

# L IS FOR LIONS

# M IS FOR MUSEUM

**N** is for **Number 10**

O is for
Observatory

**P** is for **PORTOBELLO ROAD**

Antiques

R is for

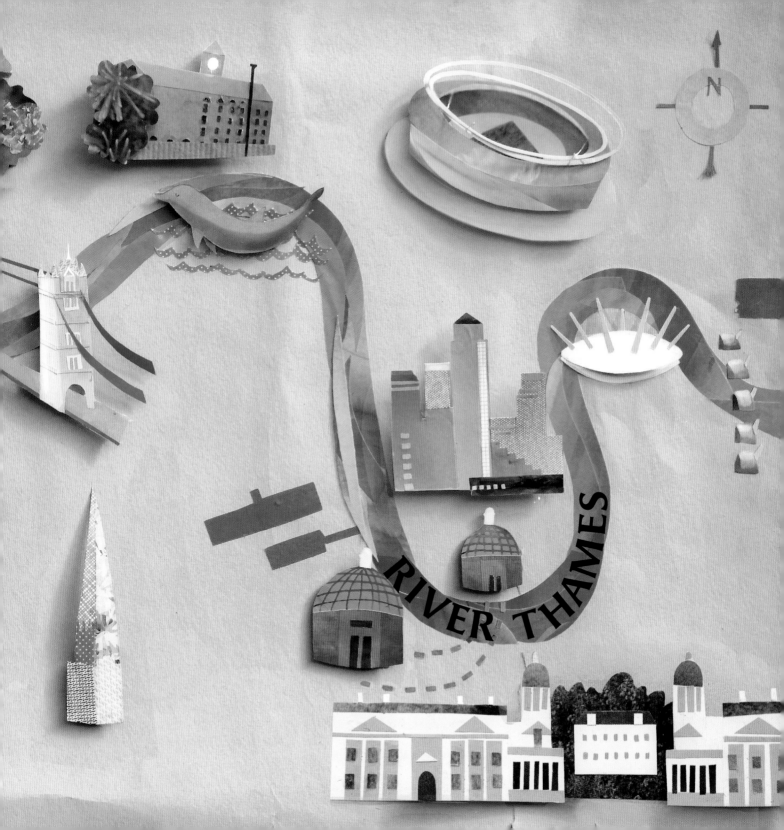

RIVER THAMES

S IS FOR ST PAUL'S CATHEDRAL

**T** is for **TAXI**

**U** is for
**Underground**

UNDERGROUND

WHITECHAPEL

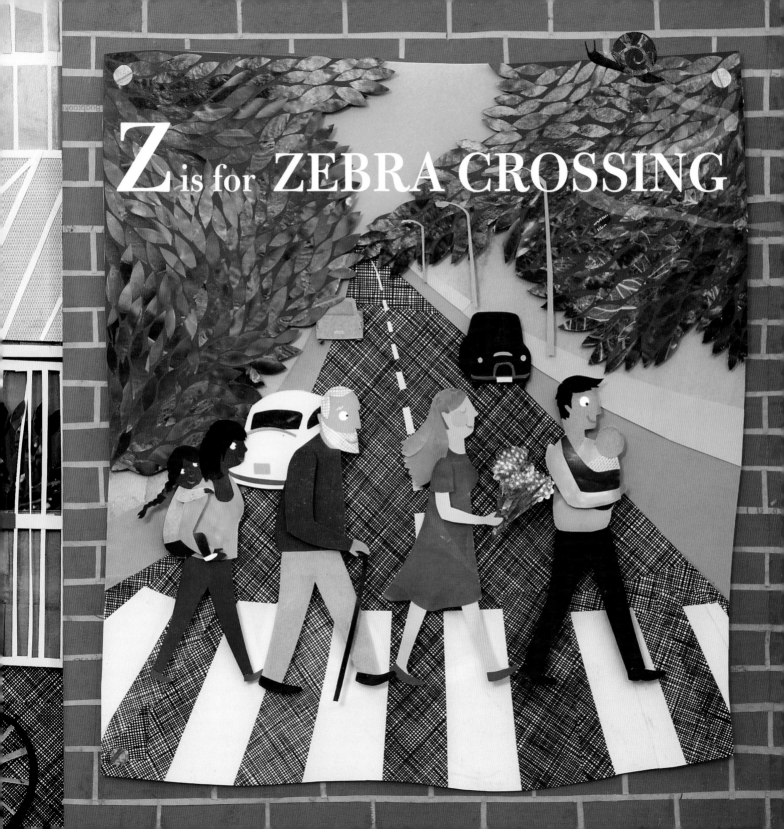

# ALPHABET GLOSSARY

 **Art** and artists are everywhere in London – in museums, galleries like Tate Modern and on the street.

 People come from all over the world to visit the city or start a new life. You can see them in action (and get a great beigel) in **BRICK LANE**.

 You have to concentrate when you're guarding the Queen. At Buckingham Palace soldiers take over guard duty in a ceremony called Changing the Guard.

 **Dick Whittington** came to London a long time ago to make his fortune. He nearly quit the city, but ended up as Lord Mayor – after selling his cat for a lot of money because it was so good at getting rid of rats!

 'Elephant and Castle' is how Londoners used to say *Infanta de Castilla*. She was a Spanish princess who married an English king, and this is where her palace once stood.

 Fashion followers worldwide check out what Londoners are wearing on the street, and what London designers are doing on the catwalk.

Of all London's tall buildings, the easiest to recognise is the **Gherkin** at St Mary Axe.

HAMPSTEAD HEATH is a great wild open space on the hills to the north of the city. Lucky Londoners live in one of the greenest cities in the world.

The **Isle of Dogs** was once an island in the heart of London's docks – and is now home to a financial centre called Canary Wharf.

The *Crown Jewels*, bling for kings (and queens) – they're all locked up in the Tower of London.

King's Cross Station is where you catch a train to the North, or to Hogwarts. . .

LIONS roam everywhere in London. There are over 10,000 statues of them, like these ones in Trafalgar Square.

If you want amazing treasures, lost civilizations, awesome technology and huge dinosaurs, then head for a London MUSEUM, like the Natural History Museum in this picture.

**Number 10** Downing Street is the address of the Prime Minister. He (or sometimes she) runs the government from here.

The Royal Observatory, Greenwich, is where the world sets its clocks. There's a Planetarium too.

Portobello Road is the most famous street market in London. From avocados to antiques, you can buy it all at Portobello.

What is the fairest way to wait for something? Queue – as everyone does here at the London Eye.

The **River Thames** links the heart of England to the rest of the world. London is the last place where you can cross the river before you reach the sea.

St Paul's is London's own cathedral. Christopher Wren rebuilt it after the Great Fire of 1666.

**TAXI** drivers in London have brains stuffed full of 'the Knowledge' – how to get you to any street you ask for.

**Underground** trains carry Londoners on a billion journeys across their city every year. Stations all have the same distinctive circular symbol.

**Villains** have always made a killing in London. Hold on to your wallet!

Wimbledon is where you'll see the All England Tennis Club and the world's favourite tennis tournament each summer.

EXiles sometimes find a home in London when their own country won't let them stay. Some, like Karl Marx, have famous memorials.

The Metropolitan Police work to keep the city safe, from their headquarters at NEW SCOTLAND YARD.

At **Zebra Crossings**, traffic has to stop to let you cross the road. The most famous one, in Abbey Road, is on the cover of a Beatles album.